Everybody knows you find your one true love as a cadet.

. . . ohhh, let's hope not . . .

Wake up. We're here.

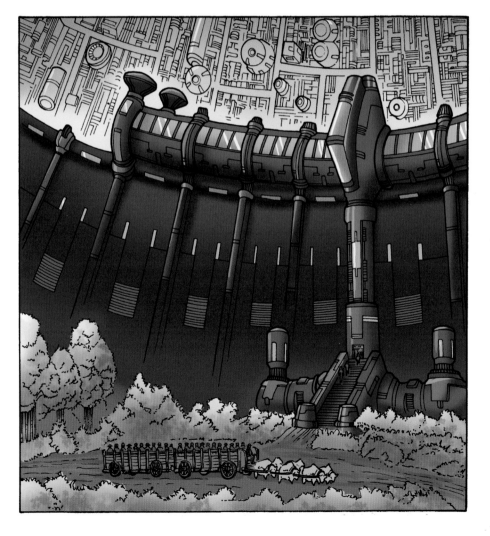

Pico!

Don't be a slow poke! Hurry up!

Let's run!

They aren't going anywhere without us!

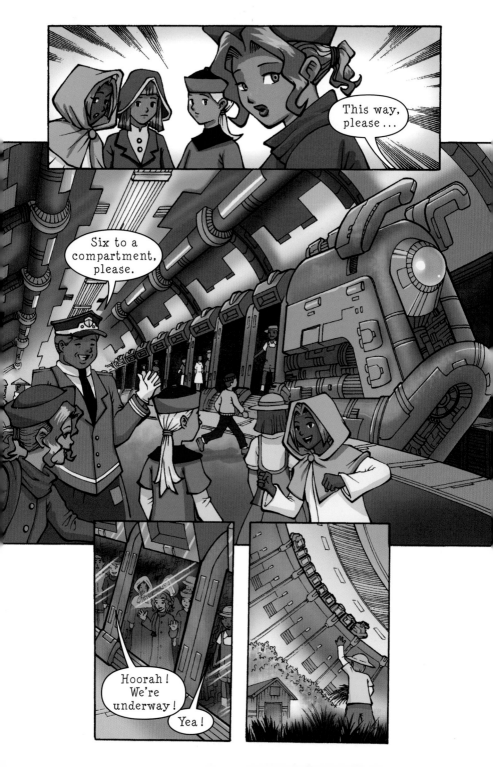

Look!
We're getting
lighter!

Well, of
course! If you
paid attention in
class you'd know
that!

Look!
There's our
village!

And
there's my
home!

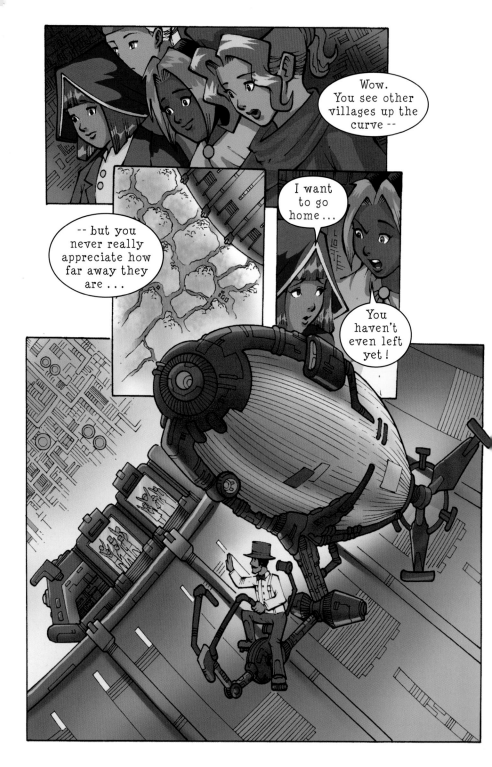

End of line! Everybody out!

And you first-timers step softly! The pull is much lighter up here!

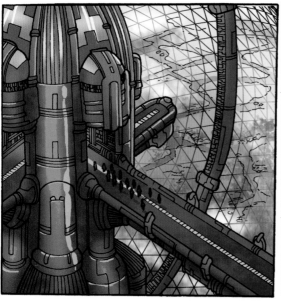

Welcome to Flight School.

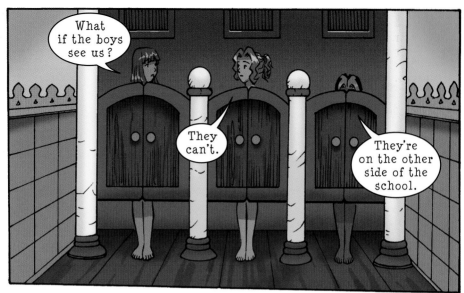

Most of us want to, but not everybody shares the same dream.

That's crazy!

All our lives we're constrained -- I want to cut loose!

You're about to get your chance, child.

Ooooooooohhh...

Didn't you learn anything in school?

Don't see the point in studying things I'm not interested in.

Still, don't we need lessons?

No. All you've got to do . . .

TOO-KOOT
TOO-KOOT

They say it takes longer on the New World.

?

The darkness doesn't come suddenly as it does here.

The technical term is "nightfall."

Night is so much different than this.

How?

Night is full of stars.

Worried? A little.

Can you tell me what it's really like?

I've told you everything I'm allowed to tell.

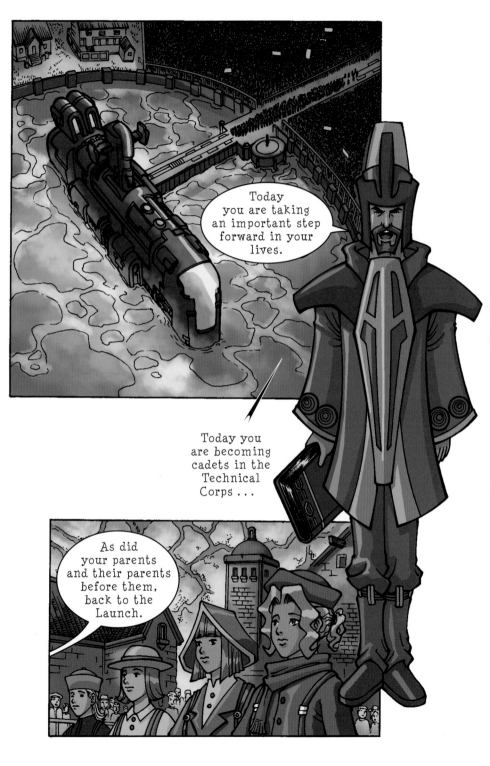

Cozane, Adam. Spinward, Dawn.

Dawn! Sit by me!

Hey! You! No talking!

You're cadets now, and cadets do what they're told!

Find your assigned seat, buckle in, and sit quietly.

Cast off!

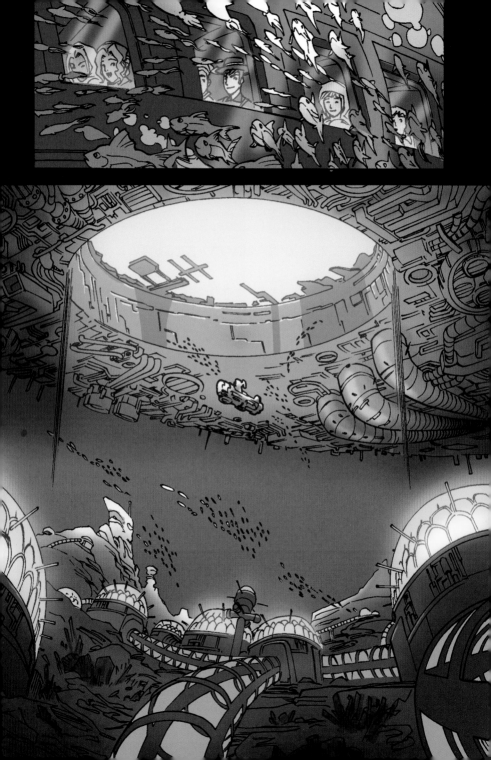

SCHLURGGGG

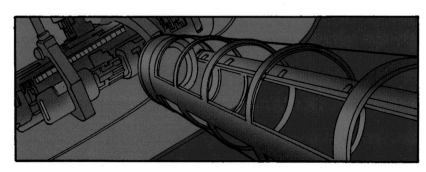

Take your seats and prepare for a period of intense acceleration.

WHOOOOOOOSH

BRAXXX BRAXXX

It means there's an oxygen leak.

Immediately drop what you're doing --

-- run to the nearest locker and grab a mask.

Once you've got yours on, help others who need masks.

You know, make sure we're all clean. No bugs.

I resent that!

Stop taking everything personally!

All our ancestors did this, so we can too. After all, it's our --

-- duty . . .

BRAXXX BRAXXX

Occasionally we've had one cadet brazen enough to rush out.

Almost always a boy, very **very** rarely a girl.

Even then, their characters are the same: Cocky little daredevil show-offs.

But you, Cadet Spinward, you're different. Your school record shows you're no daredevil.

In fact -- and I quote -- you're cited as "modest to a fault."

So tell me, why did you rush out?

I promised to obey orders.

You told me to run and get a mask if I heard the alarm.

You obeyed orders ?!?!? **Ha!** That's rich!

Daredevil show-offs do have their uses. At least they show initiative.

But you, you're the first one who ever acted contrary to her nature --

-- because she promised to obey orders!

Usually when a cadet passes this test, we appoint him --

Dawn!

Hey, it's Captain Spinward!

Pico, where's your corps etiquette? She's our captain -- treat her with respect!

In here I'm just plain ol' Dawn.

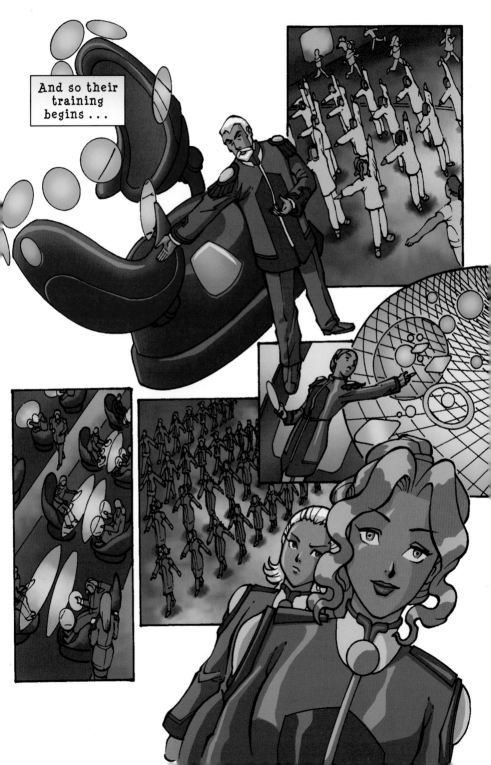

Very nice!
Did you have
access to a
terminal in the
Colony?

No, I
just read all
the computer
books at our
library.

Well,
you seem to
have a natural
aptitude for
it.

Want to be
moved to an
advanced
class?

Yes,
ma'am!

Ma'am, why can't we have computers in the main Colony?

You do have them.

Only in hospitals and emergency stations. Why?

It's a matter of resources. The Colony can't make computers for everyone.

...oh ...I see ...

I hope you're not terribly hungry, Captains Cozane and Spinward.

I am.

No, sir.

Well, it won't hurt you to eat a little later. Come with me.

How would you like to come Outside with me?

Now ?!?!?

Right now ?!?!?

Our class isn't scheduled to go Outside for another month.

True ...

Part of being a leader is going first.

Yes, sir!

... but as captains you should become experienced before your classmates.

As captains, you're a study in contrasts. Cozane, when you're the best, you're the very best ...

... except when you're the worst ...

Spinward, you're dependable and consistent but not particularly exceptional.

Sorry, sir . . .

Don't be sorry! The two of you balance each other out!

And frankly, we don't know which kind of cadet we'll need!

A hundred cycles ago, we entered the New Home system's comet cloud.

This way.

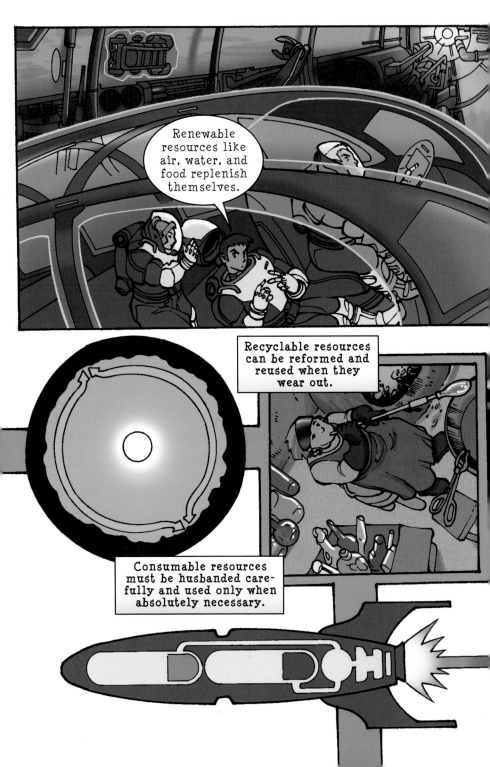

Most people don't realize it takes consumable resources to recycle.

And not all materials can be recycled indefinitely.

We're nearing the New World and our consumable resources are running out.

If we don't successfully transplant the Colony soon, we never will.

Upon entering the comet cloud, the Technical Corps's duties increased.

We had several small collisions with chunks of orbiting ice. Nothing serious.

Then we encountered something we never expected to find...

The R.A.T., sir?

Apparently, to kill every human that gets in its activated sights!

What does it want?

Isn't it just an anomaly, sir? We haven't seen any others.

We certainly hope so!

One of them was hard enough to subdue.

And so far, there's only been the one encounter a hundred cycles ago.

But if there **are** more, we can ill afford to let them disrupt the Colony!

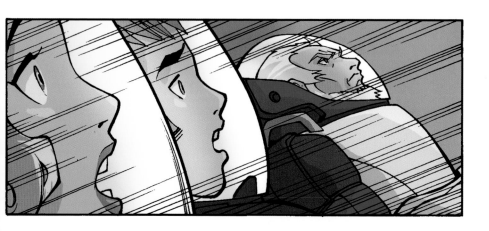

TRANSLATION NOTES:
Colonists' Names

As the language spoken by the Colonists is completely
dissimilar to any spoken on Earth in the 21st century,
it's been a challenge to the translators as to how to
properly interpret the given and family names of the
Colonists.

Since rendering them phonetically would often result
strange and wholly unfamiliar names that contemporary
terrestrial readers might have difficulty following, it
was opted to translate family names whenever possible
and given names only when there was an obvious
parallel.

Thus given names like "Bika" and "Pico" remain while
"Dawn" and "Adam" were translated.

Family names are more problematic. To begin with,
none of the original Colonists' family names survived
more than a few generations past the Launch. Their
descendants, no longer tied to the world that spawned
The Colony, allowed the old family names to fade away
and be replaced by newer names that related to their life
aboard The Colony.

For another, there is no set or rigid pattern as to what comes first, family name or given name. A Colonist may use either form at any given time. Since records are kept not based on names or an arbitrary identity number but rather on each individual's specific genetic code, maintaining a consistent pattern has not been necessary. In a formal setting, a person may be introduced first by their family name, then by their given name; in an informal setting it often is the other way around.

Tracking a person via genetic code also removed the need to use family names to trace lineage. As a result it is not uncommon for three generations to have three different family names, or for one family to have members with different family names. Indeed, it is not unheard of for new families to choose a new family name for themselves, particularly if they have relocated or chosen a new vocation.

However, again this is not a uniform practice. While a family that runs a bakery might be known as "the Bakers" in The Colony's language, it's not uncommon for a descendant who isn't a baker to be referred to as "of the Bakers." Rather than translate this as "O'Baker" or "de la Baker," and thus imply a cultural link that isn't there, we have opted to use the simplest translation.

Typically family names in the Colony are based on occupational specialty, location, or some notable piece of family history. "Miller," "Baker," "Potter," etc., all have easy translations into contemporary terrestrial languages. "Spinward," "Upslope," "Forward," etc., refer to directions within the Colony and may be translated without too much difficulty.

Complications arise when a family might be called "the Upslope-Bakers." Connecting the two names with a hyphen implies two separate families linked by marriage in many contemporary terrestrial cultures; no such implication exists in the original. Depending on how common the name is, our translators have opted to either simplify such names to "Upslope" or "Baker" or else leave it in its original language.

One note regarding Adam's attempt to hide his identity on page 25 by calling himself "John Smith." Adam was giving an extremely common Colony name in the hopes of escaping punishment. It was decided that "John Smith" was the closest corresponding name as it is common but not as obviously phony as "John Doe."

In fact, a more literal translation of what Adam said would have been "Farmer John" but our legal department suggested it would be a wise idea not to mention another company's trademark in the story.

MAKE THE JUMP TO OUR WEBSITES!

www.SerenityBuzz.com
www.GoofyfootGurl.com
          and
www.RealbuzzStudios.com not only talk about
Serenity and the Prayer Club but also upcoming new
series from Thomas Nelson and Realbuzz Studios like
GOOFYFOOT GURL and many, many more!

Make sure you visit us regularly
for advance news, fun facts, downloads, contests
and challenges, as well as online shopping!

Can you make a video?
Do you have a recipe?

Exciting new contests
coming soon to
www.RealbuzzStudios.com!

Looking For

 **Serenity** tm Swag

Or

 **Goofyfoot** tm Gear ?

Check out our online shop at
www.RealbuzzStudios.com
www.SerenityBuzz.com
www.GoofyfootGurl.com
www.GoofyfootGuy.com
[Protoypes shown; final product may differ slightly.]

ERS

ω

Sakai
z Studios
uen and
r helping out in a pinch!

Copyright © 2008 by Realbuzz Studios, Inc.   ISBN 9781595544162

Published by Thomas Nelson, Inc. Nashville, TN 37214 www.thomasnelson.com

Library of Congress Cataloguing-in-Publication Data
Applied For

Hubble and Spritizer space telescope images courtesy
NASA/JPL-Caltech.
    "Your tax dollars at work!"

Scripture quotations marked NCV are taken from
The Holy Bible, New Century Version®. NCV®.
Copyright © 2001 by Nelson Bibles.
Used by permission of Thomas Nelson. All rights reserved.

Printed in Singapore.
5 4 3 2 1

VISIT **COUPLERS** AT
www.RealbuzzStudios.com